Tales
from
SAN

D1039999

The Green Monster in Left Field

by Dan Gutman

Illustrated by Robert Papp

AN
APPLE
PAPERBACK

SCHOLASTIC INC.
New York   Toronto   London   Auckland   Sydney

Thanks to Kazuo Sayama

ISBN 0-590-13761-1

12 11 10 9 8 7 6 5 4 3 2   8 9/9 0 1 2/0

Printed in the U.S.A.   40

First Scholastic printing, May 1997

To Eva Moore

THE MEDFORD MAULERS

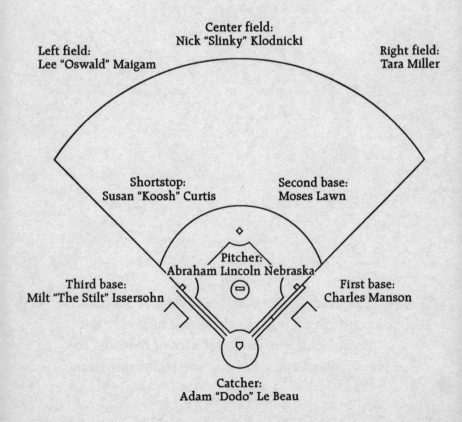

Left field:
Lee "Oswald" Maigam

Center field:
Nick "Slinky" Klodnicki

Right field:
Tara Miller

Shortstop:
Susan "Koosh" Curtis

Second base:
Moses Lawn

Pitcher:
Abraham Lincoln Nebraska

Third base:
Milt "The Stilt" Issersohn

First base:
Charles Manson

Catcher:
Adam "Dodo" Le Beau

Hōmuran!

With the *ping* of the bat, I could tell the ball was sailing over my head in left field. *Hōmuran*, I thought to myself. That's "home run" in Japanese.

It was the last inning and my team — The Medford Maulers — had a one run lead. A homer would tie the game. I wanted to catch that ball. Badly.

Coach Tucker told us there are two things an outfielder can do when a baseball is hit over your head. One of them is really smart. The other is really dumb.

The dumb thing is to backpedal. That means you run straight backwards as fast as you can.

Backpedaling is dumb for a lot of reasons. You have no speed running backwards, for one thing.

1

You're off-balance. You can't jump. You can't see where you're going.

Usually, you stumble back and fall on your butt while the ball lands behind you. Everybody laughs. Even your teammates.

The smarter way to handle a ball hit over your head is to turn your body *sideways* in the direction the ball is hit. Then you run sideways, crossing your legs with each stride and keeping your eye on the ball the whole time. That's what I did.

I ran back as fast as I could. I waited until the last possible moment to jump. Then, with every ounce of energy my legs could generate to push me off the ground, I leaped for the ball, extending my glove as high over my head as I could reach.

A Face in the Distance

Let me back up a little. It's kind of rude when people meet you but don't introduce themselves, isn't it?

My name is Lee Maigam, but everybody on the Maulers calls me Oswald. I was born ten years ago in Tokyo. That's the capital of Japan. When my father's computer company transferred him to their office in Medford, Oregon, my whole family moved with him.

Japan is crazy about *yakyu*. That's what we call baseball. I learned how to play in Tokyo. When we moved to Oregon, I tried out for the Little League and was chosen by the Maulers.

3

We are a very good team. Not quite as good as my team back in Japan, but very good.

Southern Oregon is forest country. In fact, Fagone Field, where the Maulers play our home games, is right at the edge of Siskiyou National Forest. It's also right near the Rogue Valley Mall. I guess that's why we're called the Maulers.

You're probably wondering why a ten-year-old Japanese boy would be called Oswald. One of my teammates, our center fielder Slinky Klodnicki, gave me that nickname. When I first met Slinky and told him my name was Lee Maigam, he immediately announced, "Well, I'm going to call you 'Oswald.'"

"Why?" I asked.

"Knock knock," Slinky said.

"Who's there?" I replied.

"Oswald."

"Oswald who?" I asked, bewildered.

"Oswald Maigam," Slinky said. With that, he collapsed into helpless laughter. I did not see the humor at all.

"Get it?" Slinky explained. "Oswald Maigam. I-SWALLOWED-MY-GUM!"

I still did not think that was very funny, but I don't always understand American humor. Especially Slinky's American humor, which is very strange and unrelenting.

In any case, from that moment on, I was known as Oswald. Like it or not. Funny or not funny.

I should get back to what happened when that ball went sailing over my head. It was kind of rude for me to interrupt the story like that. I apologize for getting off track. I also apologize if I use Japanese baseball words from time to time. If I forget to translate them, there is an English/Japanese baseball dictionary in the back of this book.

Oh, and I also apologize for apologizing all the time.

So, as I was saying, I leaped for this shot over my head with every bit of energy I had. But it wasn't quite enough. The *bēsubōru* — the baseball — ticked off the top of my *gurōbu* — my glove — and kept right on going.

That wouldn't be so terrible, but Fagone Field doesn't have an outfield fence to stop the balls. It *used* to have one, but a few years ago some kid jumped for a ball, hit the fence, and broke his arm. So they tore the fence down. Now when a ball sails over an outfielder's head, it goes into the woods.

The ball is still in play when it's in the woods. You can chase it. But it's usually a sure homer. The batter will almost always make it around the bases by the time the outfielder gets to the ball.

But as I chased the ball into the woods, I figured, what do I have to lose by trying? It was the last inning. The batter was a fat kid, and a slow runner. My teammates were good fielders. Maybe we could nail the kid at the plate if none of us dropped a relay throw.

The ball had come to a stop at the base of a tree. I grabbed it and turned around. My teammates were lined up for relays, just like Coach Tucker had taught us.

I threw the ball to Slinky, who plays center field. We call him Slinky because he has this strange ability to make his neck go up and down like it was a Slinky. I have no idea how he does it, but it's pretty amazing to watch.

Slinky whipped the ball to our *shoto* — shortstop — Koosh Curtis. Her real name is Susan, but we started calling her Koosh one day when somebody noticed that her new hairdo looked like one of those Koosh balls. You know, the toy made of rubber strands sticking out on all sides?

By the time Slinky got the ball from me and Koosh got the ball from Slinky, the runner had rounded third and was chugging home. It looked like a *ranningu hōmā*, or as you say in America, an inside-the-park home run. The fat kid's teammates were cheering him on, but he was huffing and puffing. Koosh wheeled around and threw the ball home.

Our catcher, Adam "Dodo" Le Beau, was waiting. When Dodo was a baby and just learning how to talk, he called helicopters "dodos." No matter how many times people told him a helicopter was a helicopter, he insisted on calling them "dodos." So after a while everybody started calling *him* Dodo.

He hates being called Dodo. But then, Dodo hates most stuff.

Dodo can catch, I'll say that much. The peg from Koosh was right on target. Dodo grabbed it. The kid tried to bowl Dodo over and knock the ball loose. Dodo simply let him run into his *mitto*,

7

then stepped aside. The fat kid dove forward and landed on the plate, like a redwood cut down with a chainsaw.

"Yer ouuuuuuut!" barked the *anpaiyā*— I mean, umpire.

It's that kind of play that put the Maulers at the top of our league this season.

After we trotted off the field and congratulated one another, Coach Tucker hurriedly gathered the Maulers together.

"I want to take a picture, kids," he said, fiddling with his Polaroid camera. "I'm gonna be thinking about you while I'm in Chicago."

Coach Tucker had to go on a business trip for a week. We had just one game left in the season. When the coach returned from his trip, we would play a one-game World Series with whichever team won the pennant in Jacksonville, which is a few miles away. The winner would be the champion of Jackson County.

"Say cheese!"

Just before Coach Tucker snapped the picture, we all started fooling around and putting two fingers up behind each other's heads.

"Hey, no rabbit ears!" Coach Tucker scolded us as the picture popped out the front of the camera. "Now I have to shoot another one."

We got serious and the coach took another photo. He handed me the first shot and kept the second one for himself.

"I've got to catch my plane," Coach Tucker said, heading for his truck. "Don't do anything crazy while I'm gone, you hear?"

As the coach's truck pulled away, Slinky and Koosh gathered around me to watch the picture develop. It started out all white, but slowly the image began to appear.

It was pretty goofy. Our *pitchā* and unofficial team leader, Abraham Lincoln Nebraska, had second baseman Moses Lawn in a headlock. Tara Miller, our right fielder, stuck out her tongue and crossed her eyes. Our first baseman, Charles Manson, had two pencils sticking out of his nostrils.

(Yes, yes, I *know* Charles has the same name as that famous lunatic murderer. Charles knows it too, and he's not very happy about it.)

"Hey, what's that?" asked Koosh, peering at the photo.

We leaned our heads closer.

On the side, off in the distance of the left field woods, was a figure.

It *looked* like a figure, anyway. It had to be pretty tall, because the woods were so far away. The background was fuzzy. But it looked almost like a big ape with a greenish face, staring intently at the camera.

I felt goose pimples on my arms. I had just been out in those woods chasing the *bēsubōru*, I mean, the baseball.

Our three heads looked up from the photo and we peered out into the woods of left field.

Whatever had been out there was gone.

Chapter 3

The Green Monster

The next day, everybody was buzzing about that blur we saw on the photo. We gathered back at the field to play the final game of the season. Because we had already won our league pennant, it wasn't a must-win game.

"It's a monster," claimed Dodo. "Let's go kill it."

"It's just an optical illusion," insisted Koosh. "The pattern of leaves in the trees makes it look like a figure standing in the woods."

"It's a monster," repeated Dodo. "I say we kill it."

"I don't know, Dodo. It looks a lot like your mom to me," snickered Slinky. Dodo got Slinky in a headlock and wrestled him to the ground.

Having grown up watching just about every Japanese monster movie from *Godzilla, King of the Monsters* to *Godzilla versus the Smog Monster*, I considered myself something of a monster expert. I explained to the team that it was highly unlikely for a monster to be hanging around a Little League field in Oregon.

"I still say it's a monster," said Dodo. "It would look cool mounted on the wall in my room."

"Hey, maybe it's a Bigfoot," said Koosh, enthusiastically.

"What's a Bigfoot?" we all asked.

"You know, Sasquatch," explained Koosh. "I did a report on it last term. Most people call it Bigfoot. It's this apelike creature that is supposed to be ten feet tall. There have been sightings in forests all over the world, but mostly in Oregon and Washington State. Its feet are supposed to be twice the size of human feet."

"Sounds like Coach Tucker," cracked Slinky. We all laughed, because Coach Tucker really *does* have enormous feet.

"That's ridiculous!" scoffed Dodo. "How would anybody know how big a Bigfoot's foot is?"

"They found tracks, Dumdum." Dumdum is what Koosh calls Dodo when she's mad at him, which is most of the time. "Scientists have never captured a Bigfoot, but there have been hundreds of sightings and lots of people believe Bigfoot is out there."

I looked toward the trees in left field where the figure in the photo had been standing. Suddenly, being a left fielder no longer seemed like the ideal position for me. It would be safer to play shortstop like Koosh, or catcher like Dodo. And preferably in a different location. Like in Japan, for instance.

"Hey, let's call it the Green Monster!" suggested Slinky. "In Boston, that's what they call the left field wall in Fenway Park."

So whatever was out there, we nicknamed it the Green Monster.

The Mysterious Throw

"Let's play some ball, kids!" boomed the *anpaiyā*.

As we took the field, I jogged out to left field . . . slowly. The thought of facing the infield and turning my back to the woods was terrifying.

In the first few innings, I kept thinking the Green Monster was going to march out of the woods at any moment and bite me. I wondered if the *anpaiyā* would stop the game if I were attacked by a monster. Maybe everybody would just drag my body off the field and keep right on playing. I imagined the newspaper headline . . .

MAULER MAULED NEAR MALL!

I wondered which of my teammates would come to my funeral. I wondered all kinds of stupid stuff.

But nothing happened, and I was able to relax as the game went on. Having already won our pennant, we didn't have to win the game, but we wanted to anyway. It was 4–3 in our favor going into the sixth inning. Six innings is all we play in our league.

The first two guys on the other team struck out. It looked like the game was just about over when our pitcher Abraham Lincoln Nebraska got two strikes on their next hitter. She was a lefty, so I knew she was more likely to hit the ball to right field than toward me in left.

But the pitch was on the outside corner and she swung a fraction of a second late. That makes a *battā* hit the ball to the *opposite* field. That is, directly toward me.

She got some — how do you say — heavy metal on it. As soon as the ball left the bat, I could tell it was a gapper. That is, it was hit in the gap between left field and center field, between me and Slinky. I turned and chased it. Slinky moved in for a relay throw.

The ball landed about ten feet in front of the woods and skittered between two trees.

My first impulse was to go after it. Maybe, I figured, I could get to the ball quickly and we could nail her at *hōmu bēsu* — home plate.

Then I thought to myself, *What are you, crazy?*

The chance of throwing the girl out was small. We had already topped our league, so this wasn't a do-or-die game.

Plus, there was this . . . *thing* . . . in the woods.

Why risk it? I stopped chasing the ball just short of the trees.

Or tried to, anyway. Actually, I slipped on a patch of wet grass and fell on my face. For a few seconds I thought I might be hurt, but I was okay. I lay on the ground for a moment to clear my head.

Suddenly, I saw a white blur — a *bēsubōru* — *shoot* out of the woods behind me. It looked as if it had been fired from a cannon. I couldn't see exactly where it had come from, and I didn't want to find out. I got up and dashed back toward the infield.

By that time, the girl who had hit the ball was

almost at third base, completing a leisurely home run trot. Her teammates were yelling and screaming for her to run faster.

"Heads up!" shouted the *anpaiyā*.

The ball zoomed over Slinky's head. It zipped past Koosh at shortstop, too, so she couldn't cut it off. The ball one-hopped about fifteen feet in front of home plate. Dodo stuck up his *mitto* and the *bēsubōru* smacked into it.

The girl was too stunned to even slide. Dodo slapped the tag on her just before her foot hit *hōmu bēsu*.

"Yerrrrrrr outtttttttttt!" barked the *anpaiyā*. "That's the ballgame. Maulers win, 4–3."

When I reached the infield, everybody crowded around me and started pummeling me on the back — our way of saying somebody did something great.

"Great throw, Oswald!" shouted Slinky.

"What an arm!" exclaimed Lincoln Nebraska.

"*Fain purē!*" said Koosh, who had learned some Japanese from me. *Fain purē* means "great fielding play."

"What are you talking about?" I asked.

17

"That throw!" marveled Koosh Curtis. "I didn't think a human being could possibly propel a baseball that far."

"I didn't throw the ball in," I explained. "I never even *touched* the ball. I fell down out there."

"Well if you didn't make the throw," asked Koosh, "who did?"

Slowly, we all wheeled around and looked toward the woods. There was a rustling of leaves, and then all was quiet.

The Hunting Party

The regular season was over, but Coach Tucker had instructed us to practice every day to get tuned up for the championship game.

A team called the Jaguars, it turned out, won the pennant in Jacksonville. We would be playing them for the championship of Jackson County the day after Coach Tucker came back from his trip. Our *pitchā*, Abraham Lincoln Nebraska, told us that his cousin played for the Jags, and that they were really good.

We spent most of the practice talking about the Green Monster. Koosh said we should call the A.S.P.C.A. That stands for American Society for the Prevention of Cruelty to Animals. Lincoln Nebraska said they would just laugh at us if we told them about the Green Monster.

Dodo said I probably made the great throw myself and was lying about it to scare everybody. I told him I couldn't throw a ball that far if I had tossed it off Mount Fuji. That's the highest mountain in Japan.

"Then I say we go out there and track the Green Monster down," suggested Dodo.

"Oh yeah?" I said. "And do *what* with it?"

"What do you think?" Dodo replied. "Kill it, of course."

Personally, I don't like killing stuff. But it crossed my mind that if Dodo killed the Green Monster, I wouldn't have to worry about the Green Monster killing *me*.

"I'm not going out there alone," Dodo announced. "I'll need a hunting partner."

Nobody wanted to go, but nobody wanted to look like a chicken either. We decided to hold a random drawing. Each of us wrote our name on a piece of paper and we put all the pieces in a baseball cap.

I didn't tell anybody, but I didn't write my own name on the paper. I wrote "Slinky Klodnicki" on it.

No way *I* was going to go out in the woods hunting Bigfoot.

Dodo mixed up the slips of paper, closed his eyes, and reached into the cap. He pulled out a slip and said . . .

"My hunting partner will be . . . Lee Maigam."

What?! Impossible! I didn't even write my name!

It occurred to me that somebody *else* had written my name. Probably Slinky, that rat! Chances were, *nobody* wrote their own name. Everybody wrote somebody *else's* name.

"All right, which one of you chickens wrote my name?" I demanded. "That was a dirty trick!"

Nobody admitted to it, of course. Everybody was snickering, so it was impossible to tell for sure who did it.

"Oswald and Dodo," Slinky smirked. "The great Bigfoot hunters."

Dodo and I each grabbed a *batto*. "If we don't come back in fifteen minutes," Dodo said seriously, "call 911."

With that, we turned and trudged off into the woods behind left field.

First Encounter

Like I said, southern Oregon is forest country. The woods get thick almost as soon as you enter them. You can be in the parking lot at the Rogue Valley Mall, and twenty feet away you might as well be in an African jungle.

Dodo and I poked around, holding our bats in front of us.

"What are we going to do if we see Bigfoot?" I asked nervously.

"Club it," Dodo replied confidently. "Club it until it's good and dead."

I had never clubbed *anything* before. I'm pretty much a pacifist. That means I don't like wars and violence and stuff. I don't even like killing bugs in my own house. I usually scoop them up in a paper cup and carry them outside to set them free.

But Dodo sounded like he had a lot of experience killing things. I figured that if we encountered a Bigfoot, I'd leave the clubbing to him.

"I guess he's not around," I said after we had hunted all of five minutes. "We'd better be getting back so the others don't worry."

"Five more minutes," Dodo said. He was walking in front of me, crouched down and looking around as if Bigfoot might be about to leap out from behind a tree any second.

A few seconds later, Bigfoot leaped out from behind a tree.

Dodo didn't see it, but I did.

He was enormous, maybe eight feet tall, and he was standing nearly erect, like a person with bad posture. He was covered with black fur. His arms were at his sides. He was slightly bowlegged and he had an enormous chest but almost no neck. It was the most terrifying thing I had ever seen.

"Uh . . . Dodo," I croaked, unable to move.

"Don't call me Dodo," Dodo replied.

"But . . ."

"Shhhh!" Dodo shushed me. "If we're going to catch Bigfoot, I want to surprise him."

"Too late," I said. "Turn around."

Dodo did. When he saw what I saw, his mouth dropped open and the bat fell from his hand. So much for clubbing Bigfoot to death.

"The G-Green M-Monster," Dodo said, his eyes wide. "We're dead meat."

"Don't move," I whispered.

It didn't look like Dodo could move if he tried. Clearly, it was going to be up to *me* to defend us. I lifted my bat slowly until it was about shoulder level. If Bigfoot charged us, I figured, I might be able to reach up and whack him in the head in self-defense. It wouldn't kill him, but at least it would stun him so we could escape.

"Don't come any closer!" I said, waving the bat.

"He doesn't understand English, stupid!" Dodo said.

"I may be stupid," I snapped at Dodo, "but I still have my *batto* in my hands."

Bigfoot didn't charge us. He didn't run away either. He stood there calmly, staring at us for what seemed like a minute.

Then, slowly, he opened up his enormous, hairy paw.

He was holding a *bēsubōru*.

Bigfoot raised the ball up over his head with both hands, the way a *pitchā* does at the beginning of a windup. Then he kicked his leg up about waist high. He strode forward, and threw the ball toward me. It zipped in front of me about chest high, right where a home plate would be if I were batting.

I stood there, too stunned to react.

Bigfoot made a gesture with his right arm and let out a loud grunt that sounded suspiciously like an *anpaiyā* calling "Steeeerike!"

I wasn't going to stick around for the rest of my at-bat.

"Run!" I screamed to Dodo. "Let's get out of here!"

I never ran so fast in my life.

Peanuts and Cracker —

"No *way*!"

When we got back to the field and told everybody what had happened, they didn't believe a word of it. Dodo and I were panting and talking excitedly, but the other Maulers were convinced we were faking it. I guess nobody wanted to believe a Bigfoot really existed.

"I *swear* we saw him!" claimed Dodo. "He was *humongous*! Ten feet tall maybe! Hairy all over! And he threw a pitch to Oswald."

They thought the last part was the funniest thing they had ever heard.

"If you saw Bigfoot," Abraham Lincoln

Nebraska said, "let's see you prove it. Take us out in the woods and show us."

"I'm not going out there again," said Dodo.

"Me neither," I added.

The rest of the team started making chicken noises. "Buck buck buck buck buck buck buck!"

"Okay! Okay!" Dodo finally said. "I'll take you to where we saw him. But I'm staying in the back."

"Me too," I agreed.

Giggling, everybody on the team grabbed a *batto*, batting helmet, shin guards, and other protective gear. They carried the bats over their shoulders like rifles and marched into the woods. They were treating the whole thing like it was a big joke. Dodo and I followed. We weren't laughing.

We got to the place where Dodo and I had encountered Bigfoot. He wasn't there. That made everybody feel *sure* we made the story up. They started goofing around, calling to Bigfoot and whistling for him like he was a dog.

"Here, Bigfoot! Here boy!"

Slinky pointed out that Bigfoot must like baseball, or he wouldn't hang around watching us play. Slinky started singing . . .

"Take me out to the ballgame,
Take me out to the crowd,
Buy me some peanuts and Cracker —"

That's when Bigfoot stepped out from behind a tree.

He was off to our left, down a hill a little ways. He had a thick log, about five feet long, in his hand. He didn't see us at first.

"The Green Monster!" croaked Abraham Lincoln Nebraska. We stopped dead in our tracks.

"*Now* do you believe me?" said Dodo, pleased with himself.

"He must be eight feet tall," estimated Koosh. "Maybe nine."

Slowly, Bigfoot turned until he was facing us. I gulped. *Everybody* gulped. Nobody moved.

"Let's get *out* of here!" whispered Slinky.

"No," said Abraham Lincoln Nebraska calmly. "He might chase us."

"We'll all run in different directions," suggested Slinky. "He can't catch us all."

"Be cool," advised Koosh. "Maybe he's friendly."

"Friendly?" laughed Dodo. "Yeah, maybe he'll have us over for dinner. *His* dinner."

"I think I just wet my pants," said our third baseman Milton Issersohn, whom we call Milt the Stilt because he's so short.

"Get a grip, Milt," said Koosh.

"And a diaper," added Slinky.

Bigfoot looked us over, slowly moving his head to scan our faces. When he got to Lincoln Nebraska, he turned and faced him.

Bigfoot tapped the log he was holding against his enormous foot. Then he tapped it against his other foot. He brought the log up to his shoulder and swung it like you'd swing a baseball bat.

He didn't look like Ken Griffey, Jr., or anything. He looked a little awkward, but he actually had a decent batting stance. Bigfoot looked at Lincoln Nebraska and grunted.

"What's he looking at *me* for?" he asked.

"He wants you to pitch to him," Koosh whispered.

"How does he know I'm a pitcher?"

"He's probably been watching us for some time from the woods."

"Are you crazy?" Lincoln Nebraska complained. "I'm not pitching to a Bigfoot. *You* pitch to him, Slinky."

"I can't pitch," said Slinky. "I'd probably bean him. Then we'd *really* be in trouble."

"Yeah, I'd hate to see this guy charge the mound," I pointed out.

Bigfoot grunted, a little more loudly. We all shook.

"*Pitch* to him, Link!" Dodo said. "Before he kills us!"

"Okay, okay, I'll pitch to him," Lincoln Nebraska said as he faced Bigfoot.

"Give him your fastball, Link," advised Dodo. "Don't try and fool him with any of your breaking stuff. Just throw him heat."

Abraham Lincoln Nebraska went into his windup and pitched the ball, a perfect strike right over where *hōmu bēsu* would be — if there was a plate out in the middle of the forest. Bigfoot brought back the log and swung it around mightily.

We could hear the swish. He was late on the swing and hit nothing but air.

"Strike one!" whispered Koosh.

Bigfoot grunted and set up as if he wanted to try again. Slinky chased down the ball and threw it to Lincoln Nebraska. He looked around at us as if he didn't know what to do next. We signaled for him to pitch to Bigfoot again.

Lincoln wound up and let it fly. Bigfoot took another big swing. He was faster this time, but he still missed by a mile.

"Strike two!" whispered Koosh.

Bigfoot grunted again, a little louder. He stamped his feet a few times and looked at the log, like there was something wrong with it. He set up for another pitch.

"This is crazy!" said Lincoln Nebraska. "I'm pitching to a Bigfoot!"

"Yeah, and you've got two strikes on him," cracked Slinky.

Lincoln Nebraska wound up again. He used the same delivery as the first two pitches, but this time he threw Bigfoot a big lollipop *chenji appu* — a change-up. The ball left his fingertips and lofted up in a high, lazy arc toward Bigfoot.

Bigfoot must have been expecting another fastball. He swung as hard as he could. He missed, of course. When he saw the ball was still hanging

34

in the air about halfway to him, he swung again. And missed again.

By that time, the ball was almost to him. He took a third cut. This time, he swung so hard, he spun all the way around and fell on his butt.

"There is no joy in Medford," announced Slinky. "Mighty Bigfoot has struck out."

Bigfoot let out a roar that made my teeth chatter. He took the log and slammed it against the ground. Pieces of wood flew in every direction as the log shattered.

Next, Bigfoot started jumping up and down, grunting and spitting and waving his arms around furiously.

We didn't stick around to see what he was going to do next. We dashed out of the woods and didn't turn around until we were on our bikes heading home.

Kill or Be Killed

When I arrived for practice the next day, I peeked through the backstop carefully before stepping out on the field. Bigfoot probably wouldn't be so bold as to walk out in the open, but you never know.

I definitely didn't want to play left field anymore. Maybe I should switch to a nice, safe indoor sport, I thought to myself. Kickboxing, maybe.

One by one, the other Maulers started arriving.

"He's out there somewhere," Lincoln Nebraska said as he plopped down on the bench next to me to tie his sneakers, "and the Green Monster is angry."

"You know, the word 'monster' doesn't mean 'bad,'" announced Koosh. "It simply means 'big.'"

"It does *not*!" countered Dodo. "It means 'evil.' You kill it."

"Maybe he's not a monster," Koosh replied. "Maybe he's really nice."

"Oh, stop being such a *girl*."

Koosh shot Dodo a dirty look. Then she punched him in the stomach.

"He wasn't angry at *us*, you know," Lincoln Nebraska commented. "He was angry at *himself* for missing the ball."

"He sure has a temper, though," I said. "You don't go throwing a tantrum every time you whiff."

"Why not?" asked Slinky. "Lots of major leaguers do."

"He's a *monster*!" said Dodo, exasperated. "They throw tantrums! What do you expect him to throw, a garden party?"

"Did you see the power of that swing?" said Lincoln Nebraska. "If he ever gets a hold of one, it might *never* come down."

"Maybe he was just in a slump," joked Slinky. Nobody laughed.

"He's no monster," declared Koosh. "He just wants to play ball."

"So let's lure him onto the field and play ball with him," said Lincoln Nebraska, half seriously.

"Are you *nuts*?" said Dodo. "Lure him onto the field and play ball? I've got a better idea. Let's lure him onto the field and *kill* him."

"Yeah, right," I said, shooting Dodo a look. "I suppose you'll club him to death with a bat?" I didn't tell everybody that Dodo had chickened out when we first encountered Bigfoot in the woods.

"No, I would get a gun and shoot him," Dodo said.

"Bullets would probably bounce right off," noted Lincoln Nebraska. "He'd probably kill *you* first."

"Shoot him?" said Koosh, outraged. "He didn't do anything to *you*, Dumdum. I think you just like killing stuff for the *fun* of it."

"Hey, what's wrong with *that*?" admitted Dodo. "Sure I love killing stuff. Especially monsters. That's what you *do* to monsters. Kill them."

"Dodo, you've seen too many monster movies," I said.

"Look who's talking. Didn't Godzilla wipe out your whole town? Isn't that why you moved here?"

Dodo says borderline racist stuff sometimes. I didn't let it bother me too much.

"Hey, if we don't kill *him*, he might kill *us*," Dodo continued. "He's a different species. We should kill him."

"With that logic, Dodo, *we* should kill *you*," cracked Slinky.

"He's got as much a right to live as we do," said Koosh.

"Here we go," Dodo said, rolling his eyes. "The animal rights lover."

"What's wrong with loving animals?" Koosh said, getting a little steamed.

Dodo broke down in fake sobbing and started to play an air violin.

"He's probably lonely," Koosh said. "He doesn't have any friends out in the woods."

"Oh, give me a break!"

"There must be others like him," said Lincoln Nebraska. "How else could he reproduce?"

"Simple," explained Slinky. "You take a mommy Bigfoot and a daddy Bigfoot . . ."

"I say we kill him so he *can't* reproduce," announced Dodo. "Then we stuff him, roast him, and eat him."

"Yum yum!" said Slinky, rubbing his stomach. "I like my Bigfoot medium rare."

"I bet he's a *friendly* monster who loves baseball," said Koosh. "He wants to be part of a team."

"Let's take a vote," proclaimed Lincoln Nebraska. "All those in favor of hunting Bigfoot and killing him, raise your hand."

Dodo was the only kid to raise his hand.

"Those in favor of luring Bigfoot to the field?"

Just about everybody else raised a hand.

I stood up and raised my hand. "All those in favor of leaving Bigfoot alone in his natural environment and pretending none of this ever happened, raise your hand."

Everybody raised their hand and threw a glove at me.

Fishing for Bigfoot

"What do you think a Bigfoot eats?" Lincoln asked as we gathered for practice the next day.

"Ten-year-old kids," Slinky suggested.

"I read that they eat fish," said Koosh. With that, she proudly pulled a fishy smelling plastic bag out of her backpack. "I caught this baby myself."

"Fish?" I asked. "Why would they eat fish?"

"Maybe they're trying to cut down on cholesterol," Slinky volunteered.

A few of us laughed. The rest of us threw stuff at Slinky.

We had a good practice. When we were finished, Koosh dumped the fish out of the bag at the edge of the woods in left field.

*   *   *

When we showed up for practice the next day, the fish was gone. We couldn't tell for sure if Bigfoot ate it, but *something* ate it. There wasn't a trace of the fish. Whatever was eating it certainly was not a sloppy eater.

After practice, Koosh left another fish on the ground, this time a few feet away from the woods in the outfield. The next day, it was gone.

Koosh left a few fish scattered around the outfield. When we showed up for practice the next day, they were all gone.

After practice, Koosh left a fish on first base, a fish on second base, a fish on third base, and a fish on *hōmu bēsu*. The next day, they were all gone.

"The trap is set," announced Koosh at the end of practice. She lugged a big bucket of fish out to the pitcher's mound and left it there. "Now let's see if he takes the bait."

We all agreed to get up as early as we could the next morning and meet at the field.

I set my alarm clock for 6:00 A.M., but I woke up fifteen minutes before it went off. I threw on

42

some jeans and a T-shirt, wrote a note for my parents, and pedaled out to the field.

As I pulled up, I could see a few bikes were already there. "Shhhh!" Koosh signaled to me. She motioned me over to the backstop, where Slinky, Dodo, and Lincoln Nebraska were crouched. I peered through the wire fencing.

There was Bigfoot, sitting on the pitcher's mound, enjoying a fish breakfast.

Field of Bad Dreams

"Okay, we got him here," whispered Koosh. "What do we do with him now?"

"Just act naturally," Lincoln Nebraska said. "Take your positions. I'll hit some fungoes."

Slowly, cautiously, we took our positions. Everybody was careful not to walk too close to the pitcher's mound, where Bigfoot was finishing off a trout. He let out a big burp.

Lincoln Nebraska tossed a ball in the air and whacked it down the third baseline. Milt the Stilt scooped it up and fired it home. Lincoln socked a *goru* — grounder — to second base. Moses Lawn snared it and whipped it back to the plate. Then Lincoln hit a few fly balls to the outfielders.

I was watching Bigfoot the whole time. He stayed on the pitcher's mound, but he turned his head and followed the flight of the ball every time Lincoln Nebraska hit it.

Then Bigfoot grunted in the direction of Lincoln Nebraska.

"He wants you to hit *him* a fungo," Koosh called.

"I wouldn't expect him to be very good with a glove," Slinky hollered to me from center field.

"Why not?" I asked.

"Well, for one thing, he can't fit one on his hand."

Lincoln Nebraska looked at Bigfoot. "Okay, big guy," he shouted. "Up the middle. Comin' atcha!"

Lincoln smacked an easy *goru* toward the mound. Bigfoot dropped to one knee, just like Coach Tucker always tells us to. He gathered the ball in with both of his enormous paws.

Then he looked at the ball, put it in his mouth, and took a bite out of it. After chewing for a few moments, Bigfoot made a face, spit the ball out, and threw the rest of it back to Lincoln Nebraska.

Everybody started clapping. Bigfoot looked around at us.

"Ug," he grunted.

"Well, he's got good hands," Lincoln Nebraska announced.

"Good *paws*, you mean," corrected Slinky.

Lincoln Nebraska took another ball from his duffel bag and hit a fungo to third, as if nothing unusual had happened.

Bigfoot actually made a couple of good plays at practice. He really seemed to be enjoying himself out there. We were able to relax a bit and forget that he might go berserk and tear us limb from limb at any moment.

After about an hour, Lincoln signaled us and we all trotted in from our positions. Bigfoot stayed on the mound.

"WE HAVE TO GO HOME NOW," Lincoln said, saying every word slowly and clearly, as if Bigfoot were a foreigner who understood only a few words of English.

"MUST GO HOME," Koosh said, picking up home plate and holding it with the pointy end up so it looked like a little house. "MUST EAT."

46

She pretended to put food in her mouth. Bigfoot stared at her.

"Ug," he grunted.

"He doesn't seem to have any language skills," noted Koosh.

"What are you talking about?" asked Slinky. "My brother's in eighth grade and he talks the same way."

"BYE BYE!" We all waved at Bigfoot like he was a baby. "SAYONARA!"

~~~~~~

"If I had a gun, I could kill him right now," said Dodo.

"Oh, give it a rest, Dumdum!" Koosh said sternly. "He's our friend now."

The team started walking away from Bigfoot, slowly and backwards. We'd had fun, but nobody wanted to turn their back on him. As we got to our bikes, Bigfoot turned around and lumbered toward left field. Then he disappeared into the trees.

"It's sort of like *Field of Dreams*," sighed Koosh.

"Yeah," muttered Dodo. "Field of *Bad* Dreams."

Dodo's Conversion

When we arrived at the *daiyamond* the next day, Bigfoot was waiting for us. We hadn't even left any food out for him. He seemed happy to see us, and we were actually happy to see him too.

Except for Dodo, of course. He said that if Bigfoot came to trust us, it would make it easier for us to sneak up on him and kill him.

Bigfoot, or "Footsie" as Slinky was now calling him, joined right into practice like he was a member of the team. As we did our stretching exercises, he got down on the grass and stretched his enormous body right along with us. He ran some windsprints alongside us in the outfield. He played *kyatchi bōru* — catch — with me, throwing the ball so hard he nearly ripped my *gurōbu* off my hand.

Then we had batting practice.

Being seven or eight feet tall, Footsie had an extremely large strike zone. But Lincoln Nebraska just lobbed the ball over the heart of the plate and let Footsie whale at it.

He looked pretty silly on those first few pitches. But gradually Footsie learned how to time the pitch. The *bēsubōru* started jumping off the bat. All our infielders moved to the outfield. They were afraid one of Footsie's line drives might take their heads off.

It didn't do any good. When Footsie got one up in the air, you didn't *need* any outfielders. The ball was *gone.* He hit one shot that probably made it all the way to Mount Ashland. And that's twenty-five miles away.

"Ape Ruth," Slinky cracked after that hit.

When he missed completely — which Footsie did about half the time — he didn't throw a tantrum anymore. He just grunted and got ready for the next pitch.

He seemed to be an all right guy, if he was indeed a guy. None of us wanted to get close enough to find out. One thing for sure though, Footsie loved *yakyu.* I mean, baseball.

50

Koosh took a Medford Maulers baseball cap and opened the back all the way to make it as large as possible. She flipped it to Footsie and he put the cap on his head. He looked pretty funny.

He smelled pretty funny too, but it was okay. We figured that if *we* didn't take a bath or shower for our entire lives, we'd smell pretty funny too.

Something unusual happened toward the end of that practice. Footsie was on the mound — his favorite position, it seemed — and Lincoln Nebraska was hitting us fungoes. Dodo was retrieving the balls as we threw them home and then handing them to Lincoln.

On one fungo, Lincoln hit a towering foul pop up between third base and home plate.

"I got it!" Dodo hollered instinctively. He flipped off his mask and dashed toward the ball.

Dodo must have forgotten that we had all parked our bikes in a group on the third base side in foul territory. The ball was on its way down, heading straight for the bikes. So was Dodo.

"Watch out!" I yelled, but Dodo didn't hear me.

He was running full speed, looking up at the sky trying to track the ball. He couldn't tell he was

51

about to crash into the bikes. We were all too far away to do anything about it.

But Footsie wasn't. He saw what was happening and suddenly raced off the pitching mound. He was surprisingly quick for such a big creature. Just as Dodo was about to slam into the bikes, Footsie grabbed him by the belt of his jeans and lifted him off the ground as if he was a bag of potato chips. The ball fell with a clang against somebody's bike.

Bigfoot lowered Dodo down on the grass gently and walked back to the mound.

Nobody said anything for a while. Finally, Dodo struggled up on his feet.

"I woulda had it," Dodo said, but not very convincingly.

"You woulda had a broken arm, Dumdum," said Koosh.

"Footsie might have saved your life, man," I added.

Dodo would never admit it, but I'm pretty sure he realized that Footsie had done a really good thing, and maybe he wasn't such a monster after all.

In any case, after that happened, Dodo stopped talking about hunting and killing Footsie and other such nonsense.

Everybody on the team — including Dodo — made an agreement not to tell *anybody* about Footsie. Scientists have been trying to track down a live Bigfoot for years. If anybody found out we had one, they would try to capture him. They'd probably run all kinds of tests on him. Maybe they'd even kill him. Dissect him. I didn't want to even think of it.

When practice was over, we all waved good-bye to Footsie and walked off the field.

"GOING HOME NOW," Koosh told him. "GO TO BED."

Footsie seemed to understand. He lumbered off into the woods beyond left field. To his home. To his bed.

The Return of Coach Tucker

When we gathered for our last practice before the big game, Footsie was like one of the gang. He was romping around the field with us like a big sheep-dog.

Just before batting practice, we saw a truck coming up the road to the field.

Coach Tucker!

Everybody stopped what they were doing. Of course, we all knew Coach would be returning from his business trip. But none of us had thought to figure out how we were going to explain Footsie to him.

Coach Tucker got out of the truck slowly. He

had a cast on his right leg. He pulled a pair of crutches out of the back seat.

"What happened, Coach?" asked Koosh, trying to distract his attention away from the field.

"I slipped in the hotel pool," Coach replied. "Broke my big toe."

"*All* your toes are big toes, Coach," joked Slinky. It was a running gag with us that the coach had enormous feet. Slinky tried to turn Coach Tucker around so he wouldn't see Footsie.

"Very funny," Coach laughed. "Hey, you know what they called me in the hospital?"

"What?" we asked.

"Bigfoot!"

We all laughed nervously. Dodo tried to push Footsie toward the woods and get him off the field. It was hopeless. Footsie weighed at least five hundred pounds, and he wasn't ready to leave.

"Who the heck is *that*?" Coach Tucker bellowed, looking out into center field.

Footsie had scooped up Dodo in his arms, put him on his back, and was giving Dodo a piggyback ride.

"Uh, who is *who*, Coach?" Koosh asked innocently.

"Who is that big guy dressed in an ape costume and carrying Dodo on his back?" asked Coach Tucker.

We all held our breath.

"Oh, *him*!" Slinky said. "Uh . . . that's Footsie, Coach. He's our new . . . uh . . . mascot!"

"Yeah!" we all agreed enthusiastically. "He's our mascot!"

"What do you need a mascot for?" asked Coach Tucker.

"To get us charged up for the big game, Coach!" suggested Lincoln Nebraska.

"Yeah," added Koosh. "The Phillies have the Philly Phanatic. The Padres have the San Diego Chicken. This is the Medford Bigfoot. We named him Footsie."

Footsie was now in the infield, tossing Dodo up in the air and catching him behind his back.

"So who is he?" Coach Tucker asked. "Somebody's dad?" He started hobbling over toward Footsie to introduce himself.

Koosh stopped him. "Coach, this is gonna sound a little weird," she said. "But we want to keep Footsie a secret. It would kind of spoil it for us if we revealed who he is. Even to you."

Coach shook his head from side to side, which is what all grown-ups do just before they mutter the words, *"These kids today."*

"These kids today," Coach muttered, sitting down on the bench. "You're crazy. Well, whatever you want is fine."

We all breathed a sign of relief.

"Great costume!" Coach Tucker called out to Footsie. "It looks so real!"

Footsie turned and looked at Coach Tucker.

"Ug," he grunted.

All You Can Eat

Coach is actually a cool guy, for a grown-up. He didn't give us a hard time about Footsie at all. In fact, he invited the whole team out for dinner that night, including Footsie.

Koosh got an XX large T-shirt and stenciled the word "FOOTSIE" on the front and "THE GREEN MONSTER" on the back. Dodo cut a big foot shape out of a piece of wood and attached a broom handle to it to give Footsie something to carry and make him look more like a real mascot.

We all piled into the back of Coach Tucker's pickup truck. There wasn't enough room, so I sat on Footsie's lap. He was trembling the whole ride to the restaurant. I guess he had never been in a car before. He had never even been out of the *woods* before.

Coach drove to Bear Creek Plaza, a small shopping center at the edge of Medford. He parked the truck in front of Hometown Buffet, a restaurant we go to from time to time. There was a big sign out front that read, "ALL YOU CAN EAT."

We settled into the seats around our table. Footsie sat in the seat between me and Dodo. After Footsie saved Dodo from running into those bikes, the two of them were acting like best friends.

I noticed that people at the tables around us were staring at Footsie, but nobody freaked out or anything. I guess they figured a *real* Bigfoot wouldn't be in a restaurant carrying a big foot and wearing a T-shirt that said "FOOTSIE" on it.

Besides, Footsie had excellent table manners. He sat quietly while Coach Tucker gave us a pep talk.

"You played a great season, kids," the coach said. "The Jacksonville Jags are a good team, but you're better, if you ask me. You deserve to win it all tomorrow. But win or lose, I want you to know I'm proud of you. Anything to add, Footsie?"

"Ug," Footsie grunted. Everybody laughed.

The waitress came over. She went around the table taking the orders of all the kids. Then she took Coach Tucker's order. Finally she turned to Footsie.

"And you, sir?" asked the waitress.

"Ug," said Footsie.

Koosh piped up. "He'll have the fish," she said.

A few minutes later the waitress brought our food. We all watched Footsie as the waitress placed the plate in front of him. He looked at the fish, leaned over, and sniffed it a bit. Then he brought his big hairy paw down on the plate and picked up the fish. He took a little nibble, thought about it for a moment, and then shoved the entire fish in his mouth.

The waitress just stared, her mouth open.

"More fish, please," Koosh requested.

Well, Footsie kept eating and eating. The waitress brought out plate after plate of fish. Finally the manager of the restaurant came over to our table, acting all nervous.

"Excuse me, sir," he said to Footsie. "We're all out of fish."

"Ug," grunted Footsie.

"The sign out front says 'ALL YOU CAN EAT,'" Coach Tucker complained.

"Yes it does," said the manager as he cleared away Footsie's plate. "And that's all you can eat."

The Big Game

It was a beautiful day for *yakyu*. It was a beautiful day for *anything* really.

Footsie was probably the first one at Fagone Field in the morning. When we arrived early for batting practice, he bounded happily out of the woods to greet us. He was still carrying his Footsie stick and wearing the T-shirt Koosh made for him.

He tried to high-five with us, but he was just too tall. It was just as well. Footsie was so strong, he might have ripped our arms off by accident.

When the Jacksonville Jags arrived, we looked them over carefully. They looked pretty good warming up. It was obvious that Lincoln Nebraska's cousin was the best player on the team. He was a big bruiser of a kid. He looked like he might be twelve, or even thirteen.

You know, I just realized I did something that was very rude. I never told you the story behind Lincoln Nebraska's name.

When I first met Lincoln, I thought his name was a perfectly normal American name honoring your great President Lincoln. Then I learned that Lincoln is the name of a town in the *state* of Nebraska.

I asked Lincoln Nebraska about it. He said his mom and dad and their brothers and sisters used to be hippies and they lived on a commune. Every time a baby was born, they named the baby in honor of a person and place they liked. That's how Link was named Abraham Lincoln Nebraska.

"So what's your cousin's name?" I asked Lincoln as we watched the Jags take fielding practice.

"Christopher Columbus Ohio," he replied.

Slinky overheard Lincoln and me talking. "Link's got another cousin," Slinky told me. "His name is Thomas Edison New Jersey."

I wasn't sure if Slinky was joking or not. With Slinky, you can never tell.

*   *   *

The bleachers were packed. I had never seen so many spectators at one of our games.

Footsie was the star of the show before we took the field. He danced up and down the foul lines pounding his chest. Then he chased one of the Jags around, while everybody laughed. Footsie didn't catch the Jag, but the kid's batting helmet fell off and Footsie jumped up and down on it until he crushed it. He even started a wave. We could tell the fans thought he was really cool.

Finally the *anpaiyā* yelled "Play ball," and we led Footsie over to our bench. It was time to get serious.

The game was close at first. Both pitchers were a little nervous in the first two innings. We got two runs, thanks to a few walks, and the Jags got one. The score was 2–1.

But then Lincoln Nebraska settled down and found the strike zone. The Jags only got a few cheap hits off him, and they couldn't get another run across the plate. Lincoln struck out his cousin twice.

Meanwhile, we were chipping away at the Jag's pitcher. A run here, a run there. We put together a string of hits in the third inning to make it

4–1. In the fifth inning, Slinky slammed a long *hōmuran* to right field. I was on base at the time, so that made the score 6–1.

It was the top of the sixth, the last inning. Lincoln Nebraska fanned the first two Jags. It looked like we had the Jackson County championship in the bag.

But you know what they say — it ain't over 'til it's over.

The pitcher of the Jags stepped up to *hōmu bēsu*. He was their last hope. Lincoln knew that if he could just get this guy out, the game would be over. He wouldn't have to face his cousin, who looked like he could change everything with one swing of the bat.

The Jag pitcher was crowding the plate. Dodo set up on the inside corner to back the kid off a bit. Lincoln Nebraska almost hit Dodo's *mitto*, but the pitch was just a little too far inside. The Jag didn't back off quickly enough, and the ball smacked him on the shoulder.

Deddo bōru, as we say. Hit by pitch. No harm done, but the *anpaiyā* waved the Jag to first base.

I didn't realize it, but Lincoln Nebraska had never hit a batter before. Like me, he's a pacifist.

67

His parents were big anti-war protesters, and they drilled into him the idea that violence was bad. So when Lincoln decked that batter, it shook Link up pretty good.

He was so afraid he was going to hit the next batter that Lincoln pitched her *way* outside. It might as well have been an intentional walk. The ump called ball four and the Jag batter dropped her bat and trotted to first. Runners on first and second. Still two outs.

"Get tough, Link!" hollered Dodo as he whipped the ball back to Lincoln a bit harder than necessary. "We're not playin' pattycake out here!"

"One more out, Link!" I shouted, trying to be helpful.

I smacked my fist into the pocket of my *gurōbu*. It had been a long season. One out and we would be the World Champions.

That is, of course, if you consider Jackson County, Oregon, the world. And my teammates do. Why shouldn't they? After all, you Americans hold a World Series every year, and the only other country invited is Canada!

As Lincoln went into his windup on the next *battā*, the kid surprised everybody by squaring around to bunt. You wouldn't expect a bunt when a team is five runs behind, especially when the pitcher looks like he's losing his control.

I guess that's why it worked. The Jag *battā* tapped the ball on the grass about halfway between *hōmu bēsu* and the pitcher's mound. Lincoln rushed in and Dodo flipped off his mask so he could pounce on the ball. Neither of them could reach it before the Jag *battā* was at first base.

Things were falling apart for us. One minute we were ready to celebrate the championship, and the next minute the Jags had the bases loaded and our pitcher was losing his stuff. We still had a 6–1 lead, but things were not looking good for the Maulers.

I looked over at the Jag bench. Christopher Columbus Ohio was putting on his batting helmet.

Two Collisions

"Force out at any base!" barked Coach Tucker optimistically. "Just one more out, Maulers!"

This was the moment of truth. The next Jag *battā* approached the plate. Lincoln's cousin Christopher Columbus Ohio knelt in the on-deck circle. An out here and we win it all. A *hōmuran* and we'd be in big trouble.

What actually happened was something in the middle of those extremes. Lincoln managed to put the ball over the plate and the Jag batter hit a high blooper behind the shortstop position. It was right between me, Slinky, and Koosh. In Japan we call it a *tekisasu hitto* — Texas hit.

I ran in from left field. Koosh ran back from her shortstop position. Slinky ran over from center field.

"I got it!" we all called at the same time.

You may not be aware of this, but it is a known scientific fact that three objects cannot all occupy the same space at the same time.

I rammed into Koosh like a truck. Koosh rammed into Slinky like a 747. The next thing I knew all three of us were on the ground, tangled up and groaning. The ball somehow dropped in the middle, untouched.

Milt the Stilt ran over from third base to grab the ball. By the time he threw it home, all three Jag runners had scored, and the kid who hit the blooper slid in just ahead of Dodo's tag.

That made the score 6–5. We still had the lead, but just barely. The tying run was at the plate — Christopher Columbus Ohio.

But the biggest problem for the Maulers was that three of us were still lying on the ground. I had banged my ankle pretty good. I didn't think it was broken, but I didn't think I could play on it either. Koosh Curtis was holding her right elbow and moaning that she slammed it into something very hard.

That must have been Slinky's head. He was knocked out cold.

In seconds, we heard the wail of an ambulance siren. Two guys hopped out with a stretcher and carried Slinky off the field. He opened his eyes and gave us a thumbs-up sign as the stretcher was loaded into the ambulance.

One of the paramedics said Slinky might have a broken leg and possible concussion. They took him to the hospital to check it out and said they'd come back for Koosh and me after the game.

Footsie hopped off the bench and carried Koosh and me off the field, holding one of us in each of his enormous paws. The crowd gave us a standing ovation, though I suspect it was mostly for Footsie.

The problem was, how were the Maulers going to continue the game? In our league, each team is allowed two substitutes in case players get injured. But we had three injured players.

Coach Tucker sent our two subs out to shortstop and center field. Then he picked up his crutches and hobbled out to talk with the *anpaiyā*, who was already discussing the situation with the coach of the Jags.

They were peering at the league rule book.

Koosh had a copy of it herself. I took it out of her backpack so she wouldn't have to bend her arm. I turned to the section titled "Substitutions."

"Each team may use two substitutes in case of injuries," the rule book read. *"In an emergency situation, the Coach or other adult associated with the team may take the place of a third injured player in the field."*

We all looked at Coach Tucker, with his crutches and his big foot in a cast. No way he was going to play left field.

Then we all turned toward Footsie on the bench. He was gnawing on a bat like it was a toothpick.

"Footsie," asked Coach Tucker, "can you play left field?"

"Ug," grunted Footsie.

Coach Tucker took that as a "yes," and tossed Footsie a glove. He looked at it. He sniffed it. Then he took a bite from the thumb. He must have liked the taste, because he took the rest of the glove and flipped it into his mouth like it was a piece of popcorn.

Footsie chomped the glove and jogged out to

73

left field. The crowd started cheering as if Babe Ruth had come back to life and decided to join the Medford Maulers.

"Footsie! Footsie! Footsie!" they chanted.

"Can Footsie catch a fly ball?" I asked Koosh.

"I don't know," she answered. "Let's hope he doesn't have to."

So here's the deal: It was the last inning. We had a one run lead. Two outs. Our pitcher was falling apart and his cousin — the Jag's best hitter — was pulling on his batting gloves.

Abraham Lincoln Nebraska versus Christopher Columbus Ohio.

The one thing I noticed about Christopher was that he had real muscles. We all have muscles, of course. But with most kids my age, you can hardly see them. When Christopher gripped his bat, you could see his biceps bulge like the guys in bodybuilding magazines. He had torn off the sleeves of his uniform, so you could really see his muscles pop.

"Hey, cuz!" Chris yelled menacingly as he dug his cleats into the *battā bokkusu* — batter's box. "I'm in the mood to go *downtown*."

74

"Not today, cuz," Link replied. "You're staying home *all* day."

They may have been pacifists who loved each other as cousins, but as opposing players Lincoln Nebraska and Columbus Ohio were fierce competitors.

Dodo trotted out to the mound for a little chat with Lincoln. I couldn't hear what they were saying, but it was obvious. Dodo wanted Link to walk his cousin on purpose and pitch to a weaker hitter. Lincoln shook his head from side to side stubbornly. I guess he wanted to end the game by getting his cousin out.

Dodo threw up his hands and went back behind the plate.

"*Me wo samase!*" I yelled. That means, "Open your eyes!"

A hush fell over the crowd. Lincoln wound up. Christopher cocked his *batto*.

Lincoln tried to nibble at the outside corner with the first pitch, but Christopher didn't fall for it. Neither did the umpire. *Bōru* one.

Lincoln tried it again with the next pitch. Same result. *Bōru* two.

Christopher wiped his hands on his pants to

75

get a better grip on the *batto*. Lincoln wiped the sweat off his forehead with his sleeve. Both of them knew Lincoln would have to put the ball over *hōmu bēsu*.

Christopher stepped into the *battā bokkusu* and took his stance. Lincoln went into his windup. The pitch came in and Christopher took a hack at it.

Ping.

The *bēsubōru* jumped off the *batto* on a line and sailed toward left field. Everyone could tell Christopher had gotten all of it. Even Footsie.

As you and I both know, there are two things you can do when a fly ball is hit over your head. The right thing is to turn your body sideways and run back, keeping your eye on the ball all the time. The dumb thing is to keep facing the infield and backpedal.

Well, Footsie did the dumb thing. He started backpedaling as soon as the ball was hit. The ball was over his head almost immediately.

Footsie reached up for it, but even at eight feet he wasn't tall enough. He stumbled backwards and fell down with a thud we could hear all the way to the bench. The ball hit the outfield grass once and skipped into the woods.

I've got to give Footsie credit. He got up right away and dashed into the woods after the ball.

Christopher took a moment to enjoy the sight of his hit. Then he tore out of the *battā bokkusu* and dug for first. He rounded the bag, being careful to tap it with his right foot. He made the turn and looked out toward left field as he headed for second.

Footsie was still in the forest somewhere, out of sight. For all we knew, he had gone home for the day.

Christopher made the turn around second base. His third base coach was waving his arms around like a windmill. That's the sign to keep going, keep running.

Christopher was rounding third when Footsie emerged from the woods. I could see he had the ball in his paw.

Footsie was over three hundred feet from the plate. He reared back, planted his back foot, and heaved the ball home. None of my teammates had bothered lining themselves up for a relay throw.

They knew Footsie liked to avoid the middlemen.

The ball made a whistling sound. The air in front of it frantically parted to let the ball through.

Christopher was more than halfway between third base and home.

"Here it comes!" Koosh screamed.

It was going to be close. Dodo set himself to block *hōmu bēsu*. The ball arrived at about the same instant as Christopher. It was a perfect strike.

Christopher barreled into Dodo, trying to prevent him from catching the ball or, failing that, knock the ball loose.

Somehow, Dodo managed to gather the ball in his glove. He and Christopher crashed to the ground. The *anpaiyā* hovered over them to see if Dodo held onto the ball.

Dodo lay on the ground, flat on his back. Slowly, he raised his mitt straight up in the air.

The *bēsubōru* was in it.

"Yerrrrrr outttt!" boomed the *anpaiyā*.

The Maulers were the champions of Jackson County. And the world.

Chapter 16

What Happened Next...

I know what you're thinking. You've seen enough monster movies in your life. You think you know how this story's going to end, right?

You think the team all loves Footsie — even Dodo — but we decide that he can't live with humans. Right? He longs to go back to the forest. He's got to return to his natural environment.

Maybe you're thinking some misguided scientists hear about Footsie and decide to capture him. But the Maulers get together and help him escape into the forest. Right?

You're thinking that the story is going to end with a teary *sayonara* at Fagone Field. The whole team will gather around Footsie. We'll have a group hug at the pitcher's mound. Maybe give him a *bēsubōru* with our signatures on it. Then he'll lumber off into the left field woods with a baseball cap on his head as we wave good-bye and dab tears from our eyes.

Right? That would make a great ending.

Well, forget it. You've seen *too many* monster movies. It didn't happen that way at all. Here's what actually happened. . . .

On the day of our big game with the Jags, a scout for the Seattle Mariners stopped at Medford on his way from California to Seattle. He saw the last few innings of the game. When Footsie uncorked that amazing throw from the woods, the scout rushed onto the field with his briefcase and whipped out a contract. Footsie ate it.

But the next thing we knew, he was walking off the field with the scout. A week later, he was playing center field and batting cleanup for the Seattle Mariners.

Footsie, of course, started tearing up the American League. He was making unbelievable throws and socking tape measure homers so far they didn't have tape measures long enough to measure them. Pitchers were afraid to face him. Fans poured into ballparks to see him. It was like the second coming of Babe Ruth.

That was a few months ago. I looked in the paper today to check the standings. The Mariners have a ten game lead in their division. Footsie has forty-four homers. And it's only July!

Everybody says Footsie is a cinch to hit seventy or even eighty home runs this season. He's going to break every hitting record in baseball history.

Footsie, of course, has become a real celebrity. An agent contacted him right after he joined the Mariners. The next thing we knew, he was appearing in a commercial for Mountain Dew.

Nike created a "Bigfoot" sneaker for "full-footed" people. Coach Tucker even bought a pair!

Footsie was on the cover of *People* magazine, which we thought was pretty funny considering he's not even a person. He recorded a rap album — all grunts. The gossip columns started reporting Bigfoot sightings — Bigfoot with Princess Di. Bigfoot with Julia Roberts.

Footsie got some bad publicity too. The press said he had a real attitude problem because he wouldn't talk to reporters or sign autographs. Of course, Footsie couldn't speak or sign his name, but that was beside the point.

To celebrate our championship, Coach Tucker organized a team trip to Seattle to see the Mariners play the Yankees. It was great. Some guy on the Yankees slammed a shot off the wall and Footsie threw him out . . . at first base. He also hit seven home runs in the game, something which had never been done in all of baseball history.

After the game, we decided to go to the player's entrance so we could say hello to Footsie. The first guy to come out of the locker room was Mickey Morgan, the Mariners' backup first baseman.

"Hey, Mickey," Koosh yelled, "can I have your autograph?"

"Get lost," he replied, pushing his way to his car.

I had heard that professional athletes could be mean, but it was still disappointing when we saw it with our own eyes. Our hopes were raised when we spotted Matt Carapelli, the third baseman for the Mariners. He was a rookie, so we figured he might be nicer.

"Matt! Matt!" shouted Slinky. "How about signing my cast?" Slinky's leg was almost healed, but he was still on crutches.

"Beat it, runts," was all Carapelli said.

We were really getting bummed out. But then Footsie's unmistakable head popped out of the locker room door. Cameras were flashing. Girls were swooning. Kids crowded all over him. It was Footsiemania.

Footsie looked different from the way we remembered him. He was wearing gold jewelry around his neck and an earring. He had on sunglasses. He had dyed his fur bright green. He walked more erect.

"Footsie!" we called out, "remember us?"

He didn't look in our direction.

"Footsie!" I yelled. "We discovered you, dude! We taught you how to play the game!"

"Ug," he grunted, brushing past us as he stepped into his limousine. It roared off into the night.

Man! That guy turned into a real . . . monster!

Note to the reader

The legend of Bigfoot, or Sasquatch ("wild man"), goes back to 1811 when British explorer David Thompson discovered enormous footprints in the wilderness near Jasper, British Columbia, in Canada. Early settlers of the U.S. Pacific Northwest made similar discoveries, and a few claimed to have actually seen the large manlike creatures. It was said that a young Bigfoot was captured in 1884.

In 1924, some prospectors on Mount St. Helens in the state of Washington shot and wounded a Bigfoot. It attacked them, and that evening the cabin the prospectors were staying in was bombarded by rocks weighing as much as two hundred pounds.

A short, fuzzy film of a Bigfoot was shot in 1967 by California rancher Roger Patterson. Some believe it is authentic. Others insist it's a fake.

"If the Sasquatch do in fact exist, they are man's nearest living relative," states *Collier's Encyclopedia*. "It is hard to believe a creature this large is still almost unknown, but harder yet to believe that all the footprints and history have been faked, and that all the eyewitnesses imagined what they saw."

Baseball translated into Japanese

Baseball was introduced to Japan by an American professor in the 1870s. By the 1930s, the game had become the Japanese national pastime.

In Japan, many baseball terms are simply "Japanized" versions of American baseball terms. "Batter" is "battā," for instance. "Pinch hitter" is "pinchi hittā." "Rookie" is "rūkī." "Double play" is "gettsū" (get two!).

Here is a list of common baseball terms and how they are translated into Japanese:

ball (as in ball one): *bōru*. The baseball itself is *bēsubōru*. The game of baseball is *yakyu*.

ballpark: *yakyjyo*

base on balls: *foa bōru*

bases loaded: *furu bēsu*

bat: *batto*

batter: *battā*

batter's box: *battā bokkusu*

batting average: *daritsu*

batting helmet: *herumetto*

beanball: *bīn bōru*

bloop hit: *tekisasu hitto*

bunt: *banto*
catch: *kyatchi bōru*
catcher: *kyatchā* or *hoshu*
change-up: *chenji appu*
curveball: *kabu bōru*
diamond: *daiyamond*
double: *niruida*
double play: *gettsū*
error: *erā*
extra innings: *encho sen*
fastball: *sokyū*
first base: *ichirui*
fly ball: *furai bōru*
foul ball: *fauru bōru*
full count: *furu kaunto*
fungo: *nokku*
good play!: *fain purē*
glove: *gurōbu*
grand slam: *manrui hōmā*
grounder: *goru*
hit and run play: *hitto endo ran*
hit by pitch: *deddo bōru*
home plate: *hōmu bēsu*
home run: *hōmuran*. A game-winning home run
    is a *sayonara hōmā*.

infield: *naiya*

inside-the-park home run: *ranningu hōmā*

knuckleball: *nakkuru bōru*

left field: *refuto*

line drive: *rainā*

manager: *kantoku*

mitt: *mitto*

on-deck circle: *nekusuto battāzu sākuru*

out: *auto*

outfield: *gaiya*

passed ball: *pasu bōru*

pinch hitter: *pinchi hittā*

pitcher: *pitchā* or *tōshu*

pitcher's mound: *maundo*

play ball!: *purē bōru*

play catch: *kyatchi bōru*

relief pitcher: *ririfu tōshu*

rookie: *rūkī* or *shinjin*

safe: *seifu*

scoreboard: *sukoa bodo*

second base: *nirui*

shortstop: *shoto*

shutout: *shatto auto* or *kanpū*

single: *singuru-hitto*

slide: *suberikooni*

slider: *suraidā*
strike: *sutoraiku*
strikeout: *sanshin*
stolen base: *tōrui*
switch hitter: *suitchi hitta*
tag out: *tatchi auto*
third base: *sanrui*
triple: *sanruida*
umpire: *anpaiyā* or *shinpan*
wasted pitch: *uesuto bōru*
wild pitch: *wairudo pitchi*

About the Author

Dan Gutman has always loved baseball, but when he was growing up he wasn't a very good player. "I was afraid of getting hit with the ball," he says. But that didn't stop him from enjoying the game and learning everything he could about it.

In the last few years, Dan has written seven factual books about baseball and one fictional story, *They Came From Centerfield*, published in 1995. He had so much fun writing the story that he wanted to do more, so he came up with the idea for this series.

In between sports stories, Dan wrote *The Kid Who Ran for President*, a funny story about a twelve-year-old who runs for president of the United States. It was published in 1996.

When he's not writing, Dan can often be found visiting classrooms, where he talks to students about baseball and writing books.